The Chronicles Of Grace

LAURA HANDLEY

WestBow Press books may be ordered through booksellers or by contacting:

WestBow Press
A Division of Thomas Nelson & Zondervan
1663 Liberty Drive
Bloomington, IN 47403
www.westbowpress.com
844-714-3454

ISBN: 978-1-9736-7653-9 (sc)
ISBN: 978-1-6642-0995-4 (e)

Library of Congress Control Number: 2019915773

Print information available on the last page.

WestBow Press rev. date: 11/16/2020

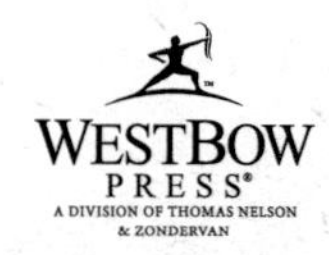

Dedicated to Sophia Grace

God's little warrior, who survived an amputation
following a 24-week gestation. Endured the loss
of her twin and mother shortly thereafter.
Placed in an orphanage in the heart of Africa at 6 weeks,
and lost her father who eventually succumbed to H.I.V.

Author, Laura Handley, met Sophia Grace while on a
mission trip to Zambia, Africa. Laura's heart was captured
by 9-month-old Sophia, so fresh from the hand of God,
who had fashioned her perfectly. Her care and upbringing
were entrusted to Ms. Handley through adoption. They
now reside in the green and fertile lands of the midwest.

To Sons of Thunder Ministries with gratitude
beyond what I could ever express.

Introduction

A torrent of frigid night air throws open the weathered shutters. An angry tempest reaches through the dark, overpowering me like a plague. Icy fingers attempt to strangle every molecule of warmth my body desperately clutches to.

Pulling my garment around me, I reach to secure the shutters as they continue to bang without mercy against the wooden frame, echoing through the solar chamber of the massive castle I call home.

The wind howls, striking my face with an arctic blast, as if in protest of being restrained and shut out.

"Ahhh," I sigh as I settle back down into the familiar crevasses and comfort of my chair.

The heat radiating from the ancient stone fireplace chases away one last shiver from this old warrior's body.

Listening to the crackle of splitting wood, I can't help but chuckle as it reminds me of an ill-tempered woman on a rainy night, piercing the silence like a stinging whip.

I tip my head back, watching in amusement as shadows of firelight flicker on cracked wooden trusses, as if the shadows have come alive, laughing with exuberance and dancing like an innocent child without concern or fear of the future.

I reach for quill and parchment as I chronicle bygone times, my attention turning to my sleeping comrade. With a soft and gentle voice, I whisper, "We fought well together, didn't we? Great battles, clanging swords, and mighty champions of truth... Dream on, my friend."

Gazing into the blazing fire, I become a bit melancholy, remembering when light became dark and the children of Elyon traded their destiny for a lie. Such somber days those were.

“Mercy, mercy, mercy,” mimics the great griffin warrior. “That’s all I ever hear. You’re like a child looking at her reflection in a mirror, only to walk away, forgetting who you are. You will never be fit to fight in Elyon’s army as long as you remain self-absorbed.”

Grace strains her voice as her lungs thirst for a fresh breath of air under the weight of the griffin’s unrelenting paw.

“Aloysius,” she whispers with a hoarse voice, “what kind of warrior could I ever be with only one leg? I can’t do anything. I’m like a discarded piece of cloth no one has use for.”

Releasing the pressure from around her neck, Aloysius shakes his head in frustration, broken feathers escaping into the wind like seedlings searching for fertile ground. He paces, carving another worn groove within the rocky summit. Abruptly he stops, kicking up dust beneath him as he turns to face Grace. Attempting a gentler tone, he clears his throat, wings tightly encased behind him.

Softening his voice and failing miserably at a smile, he speaks. “Grace.” He pauses. “Young novice.” He pauses again, as if to draw attention to his sad attempt at showing patience. “Your enemy will stop at nothing until he crushes your heart and rips your soul with his teeth. He will laugh as he spits you out and watches you shrink from all you could have been into nothingness.”

Unable to hold his frustration at bay, Aloysius explodes like thunder, enraged and exasperated. “Is that what you want, Grace? Eternal suffering?” Bringing his eyes a mere blink away from hers, he whispers accusingly, “I think you do.”

Tears well up in Grace’s eyes as she throws herself on the ground with flailing arms. “l can’t, I can’t,” she cries.

With a powerful rush of indignation and annoyance fueled by adrenaline, Aloysius soars into the sky, over the mountains, and through the valley—faster and faster until a streaming rainbow of color is all that can be seen.

Grace stands and wipes her tears, awestruck by the magnificent display of power and ferocity in this champion warrior.

With a forceful surge of wind and a rustle of feathers, Aloysius takes his stance once again before his charge. The dust beneath Grace swallows her whole as Aloysius hides his amusement.

Spitting sand out and wiping it from her eyes, Grace tries to focus once again on her mentor. Speaking softly with a hint of sarcasm, she asks, "Can I do anything else to make your day, Aloysius?"

Neria is always a welcome interruption. It is said of this beautiful and most tender of all creations that she carries the tears of broken hearts to the feet of the Creator.

Some say she loves and shows mercy as she herself has been loved and shown mercy.

No one could mistake her gentle voice, but today is different as she speaks with urgency, which is quite unlike her.

"Grace," she beckons, "come along. We must make haste if we're to make it back to the castle in time."

Taking Aloysius into her confidence apart from listening ears, Neria

unfolds the horrific drama that has taken place in the lands of Elyon, their Creator.

Panic and dread fill Aloysius's heart. He pauses for a moment, foreseeing the ramifications of such malicious vengeance.

Knowing his pain, Neria softens her voice. "Aloysius, I'm afraid there's more. The Creator has summoned Grace to be used as his voice, placing her at the center from whence this atrocity came."

"She is far from ready," Aloysius says, raising his voice. "She is still governed by her emotions, does not concentrate, and wells up with puddles of water deep enough to drown in."

"Perhaps what the Creator wills requires trust at times," Neria affirms, glancing at Grace, "even if we don't always understand. Elyon grows weary at the behavior of His creations. They have imprisoned our good king and lifted themselves up like a shrine. Their pedestal is built with pride, false humility, and self-righteousness." Neria pauses, her eyes filling with tears. "They are looking to Prince Amoz to guide them."

Aloysius's hair stands on end as he roars with passion and fury. "My heart burns within me to once again lead Elyon's warriors into battle, crushing the heads of all who would oppose His sovereignty."

Neria attempts to soothe Aloysius's heart. "You are and always will be remembered as the greatest of all warriors. Your valor in the midst of warfare is incomparable. But Elyon, knowing your heart, has called you into a different kind of war, hasn't He?"

Nodding, Aloysius acknowledges the truth in her words. Blinking so as not to show, Neria emotion, the hardened warrior standing before her is now a broken warrior who prays, standing in the breach for others.

Neria readies their departure, lifting Grace and placing her securely on her back. With one last glance at her old friend, she dips her head out of respect, turns, and takes flight.

Aloysius disappears into the dark and dismal cave he refers to as his sanctuary. He falls and weeps with raw emotion, taking on himself the anguish of his Creator. To have Elyon's own children turn their backs on all He has sacrificed for the pleasures of sin and unrighteousness ravages the spirit within him.

As in time past, they will most certainly fall beneath the weight of their choices, calling out to the Most High only when no one else will listen. Elyon simply longs to love a masterpiece of His own making, to delight in His children's praises, to comfort them in trials, and to call them friend and beloved. And when the time comes, He longs to lead them into His presence for all eternity.

With his heart moaning and in distress, Aloysius pleads with the Creator to push back the forces of darkness, to dispel spirits of pride, and to let loose the bonds of hypocrisy, which run so deeply in the hearts of His creations.

"l beseech You once more, oh faithful and true, have mercy on these, Your children, who become so easily entangled in the web of false doctrines and self-love. Arise from Your throne as the great and mighty lion of Judah You are and prepare Your army for war." Aloysius groans so deeply beyond words that even the angels weep.

Neria and Grace make their way through what was once a majestic valley. It had verdant hillsides, blades of grass that glistened like emeralds under the golden rays of the sun, and fields of flowers, whose beauty surpassed that of kings. But now, as if looking into a murky sea, the ambiance that once reflected like crystal now lies covered with anger, malice, slander, and wicked speech. An eerie oppression holds the creations captive by their own will.

"There it is," Neria discerns, "that dark and threatening heaviness that hangs in the air like a tenacious and abiding storm, preparing to unleash in all its fury."

Neria isn't the only one captured by a sense of doom. Childlike curiosity tempts young Grace to steal a look behind her. Eyes wide, she gasps in horror, crouching down into the safety of her friend.

"Pythius!" Neria whispers to herself. "He's here. I know it!"

For ages he was thought of as a legend, passing down from the old to the young. Mothers threatened their young to stay within Elyon's borders, or Pythius would snatch them away. This warning became a believable incentive for the young to obey. Fables of a creature who reveled in darkness, spewing out misery and death, caused hearts to fall faint at the very thought of him.

But since when do fables unleash pain and destruction? Neria wonders.

Approaching their citadel, guarded by Elyon's warriors, both seen and unseen, Neria increases her speed, swerving to the right. She spirals down through the portico, beating her wings with force and trying to outmaneuver her formidable foe.

Grace screams as the heat from Pythius singes her skin. "Neria, I can't take anymore." She tries to speak between Pythius's powerful surges of fire. "I'm barely hanging on. Can we please hide in the forest until this is over?"

Neria, ignoring Grace's request, speaks with rushed, undaunted fervor. "Listen carefully, Grace, as I cannot repeat myself. Elyon has chosen you to speak with Prince Amoz. Elyon will instruct you on what you must say."

Grace freezes, eyes wide, fear running through her veins. Sickness overcomes her. The very thought of Prince Amoz brings images of horror and panic to any creature who dares speak his name. Something evil captured his heart long ago, silently waiting to unleash its wrath on any who oppose him.

"Neria, I—" Grace pauses to find words. "I can't do what you ask. I was not created for such tasks. I'm sure there's someone else who—"

Neria sternly interrupts, "Grace, I am not the one bidding you to do this. Will you oppose Elyon? He is the one giving charge, not me."

Knocking on the castle door and requesting an audience with the prince doesn't seem like the smartest way to deliver any kind of message, especially a decree coming from the throne of Elyon.

Trembling with apprehension, Grace knows her only chance of survival is to beseech King Tobiah for mercy and a way out of her imminent demise.

"The only way to the king is through this window," Neria shouts above the clamor.

Before Grace has a chance for a rebuttal, Neria throws her into the air, hoping she has calculated the right distance.

A very embarrassed young girl looks up into the steel-blue eyes of the king.

Hiding his grin from his anticipated visitor, King Tobiah offers his hand. Searching the face of his new visitor and seeing nothing but fear, the king offers his warm smile, which is capable of melting the coldest of hearts. He extends his hand with compassion, offering assistance to posture herself.

"To whose honor must I thank for this charming little bird, who fell into my palace?" the king softly asks.

Being quite humbled in his presence, Grace answers with apprehension. "Why … to the Creator? … I guess—" Grace looks down at the dusty and broken wooden floor, which so reminds her of herself. "Why He chose me, I have no idea."

With an encouraging touch and a heart overflowing with love, King Tobiah replies, "I've learned the wisdom in not questioning the Creator's ways but simply trusting that how He chooses to work cannot be wrong."

Trying to maintain balance with one leg, Grace speaks with embarrassment as she stares at what she believes to be her disfigurement. "It's hard to trust that I could ever be anything more when all I see is one leg. I'm afraid I'm no use to anyone," Grace mumbles to the king.

“Perhaps it’s time to start looking at yourself from a higher point of view.” The king speaks with confidence.

He gently moves Grace in front of an ancient but seemingly magical mirror. It is capable of reflecting who we are in the Creator’s eyes apart from our own inaccurate opinion of ourselves.

If not for the recognizable features staring back at her, Grace would never have imagined herself any more than a lopsided girl delivering water to Elyon’s strong and mighty. Standing before her is a warrior, whole and complete, with determination and purpose resonating through every fiber. She is set free from the misconceptions she has believed about herself. Grace vows that one day she will become this warrior.

“No, Grace,” the king corrects, “this is how Elyon sees you *now*. You must hold on to this truth, even when you walk through the darkest of valleys.”

Disbelief fills her heart.

Grace confides to the king, sharing thoughts of unworthiness and opening up about the times she turned her back on Elyon and walked away.

“l am not intimidating to look upon. I’m not an orator, and I am way too emotional.” She pauses.

“All I have is my heart, which longs to be filled with the love of Elyon, but I’m just not worthy.”

King Tobiah smiles as he takes her hand comfortingly as a father might for a young child.

“It’s your heart, Grace, that sets you apart, for there are many who have grown cold and unresponsive to the Creator’s call. If the chosen of Elyon continue to sleep with a blanket of complacency, they will awaken only to find themselves sleeping with the enemy.”

Grace asks, “What does any of this have to do with me?”

“You’ve been chosen. Your days are ordained from the beginning of time for this moment,” King Tobiah explains. “You are to be a vessel illuminating the darkness that has shrouded our land, giving His children hope, and showing Prince Amoz there is one coming who is greater than he, who is worthy of all praise. Our Creator is calling for all His children to lay down their pride and rebellion and stand for—”

"Ha!" Grace explodes with laughter. "You think I'm going to face off with the prince? Even if I did, I would be too afraid to speak. My words would get all mixed up, and I stutter when I'm nervous. I just can't do this. It's way too much to ask of me or anyone."

With the authority of a king and the humility of a servant, King Tobiah persists. "Elyon doesn't give the hardest battles to his strongest warriors, Grace. He creates his strongest warriors through life's hardest battles."

"I just don't know what to do," moans a sullen and indecisive Grace, unaware of the spiritual battle raging inside her. "There's part of me that wants to do right, to stand strong and be a warrior for Elyon, but then fear takes over, bringing me back to the reality that I'm not much of a warrior at all."

"Never take counsel from your fears, child. Who you are in the Creator and what you feel can be two opposing forces that will wage war if you let them. You must choose each day to live with discipline or live with the pain of regret at what you could have been."

Grace feels the quiver in her jaw and the burn in her eyes that comes before the tears. "I'm so tired of being me," Grace weeps. "I'm broken physically and emotionally."

King Tobiah pauses, looking deep into her misty brown eyes. "The Creator uses broken hearts and bodies, Grace, so His light—and His light alone—can shine through for His glory and righteousness. Trust Him, Grace."

Submitting to the gentle nudge of the Creator, Grace offers herself unreservedly. A sudden warmth pours over her as if a flask of precious oil has been broken just for her. A pure and holy love surges through her spirit like nothing she has ever experienced before, breaking bonds of fear that held her captive and giving her the will to trust Elyon's purpose for her life now and forever.

No parting words are necessary between the king and this new warrior. In silent affirmation, they both know it is time.

Reveling in his self-appointed monarchy, Prince Amoz rules with fear and manipulation. Never again is the Creator's name to be spoken. Doing so would cause unbelievable mayhem and torture for transgressors and their families.

With the aid of her sword, Grace makes her way to the great hall. There is a captivating stillness in the room, as if a presence greater than she has been ushered in. Those in court wait in hushed silence for the judgment of the prince, for no one is allowed in his presence bearing any form of physical imperfection.

With repulsion and curiosity, the prince wonders at the boldness of one so pathetic.

Eyes fixed on the unseen, Grace takes her stand. "I'd like to speak with you, lord, on behalf of the king."

Coming out of his throne in anger, Prince Amoz roars, "The king! He is to be exiled for crimes against the throne, the people, and most importantly, me."

Grace chimes in before Prince Amoz can speak another word. "I'm not referring to your father, sir. I'm speaking of our Creator, Elyon, in whom there is no equal."

The court gasps. Eyes fix on the prince as everyone awaits his pronouncement of torture on this foolish girl.

Grace continues with boldness and resolve. “You have been blinded by your own bitterness and unforgiveness, leading the children of Elyon into darkness. But there is no darkness the light of Elyon cannot reach. Mercy is extending its scepter, calling those to awaken from their slumber and to be all they were created to be. You, Prince Amoz, face a greater judgment, for through you this darkness has come.”

Fuming with anger, the Prince screams, “How dare you lecture me. I have done nothing but given these wayward children the freedom to become their own gods, as they have always desired to be. Once their souls are submitted to me, they will blindly walk off any cliff of my choosing, falling headfirst into the eerie blackness of the abyss. Then and only then will my vengeance be satisfied.

“As for you,” the prince boils with anger like molten fluid rock that issues from a volcanic vent, the prince passes judgement on Grace. Towering over her in an attempt to intimidate he continues.

“Those inward parts Elyon so delicately fashioned will wither away with disease before their time, becoming nothing more than fodder to satisfy the cravings of the ominous and apocalyptic beast. You will be tormented physically and mentally cursing the name of Elyon and the day you were born. The name, Grace, will become as a reproach in all of creation and for all eternity. You will become nothing, because, you are nothing.”

With a pause the prince waits, expecting Grace to crumble with fear and fall to the floor, pleading for mercy, but he beholds only strength.

"Oh," he continues sarcastically, "do you think this God of yours will rise up on behalf of one broken child?" Prince Amoz laughs at the thought of it. "He would be a bigger fool than you to wage war against me."

The prince mockingly raises his hand above his eyes, looking around his court. "Where are your generals? Where are your armies? With what do you fight—one leg and a rusty, old sword?"

Prince Amoz's face contorts wickedly as he spews out insults. "Why, you're nothing but one pathetic cripple—and a girl at that."

Then came a mighty rush of wind and an explosion of thunder. Lighting ripples through the court as the people shield their faces.

Grace raises her sword as purity and brilliance resonate through every living creature. “Prince Amoz,” Grace says with boldness. “Look,” she proclaims with convictions, “and see the armies of God. With them do I stand and battle for truth.

“I saw heaven standing open, and there before me was a white horse whose rider is called ‘Faithful and True.’ With justice He judges and makes war. His eyes are like a blazing fire, and on His head are many crowns. He has a name written on Him that no one knows but Himself.

“He is dressed in a robe dipped in blood, and His name is the Word of God. The armies of heaven are following Him, riding on white horses and dressed in fine linen, white and clean. Out of His mouth comes a sharp sword, with which to strike down the nations. He will rule them with an iron scepter. He treads the winepress on the fury of the wrath of God Almighty.

On His robe and on His thigh He has this name written: KING OF KINGS AND LORD OF LORDS.”

(*NIV*, Revelation 19:11–16)

The sky, red from fire, is filled with black smoke, blinding the eyes of Neria and Pythius. Relying on only their senses, they tear into the air with talons, hoping to find the meaty flesh of their foe.

Neria roars in pain, whipping her tail to her right flank, hoping to break loose from Pythius's front talon, which slices into her already-bloodied flesh.

Pythius pulls back hard exposing muscle and bone leaving Neria physically impaired. Releasing his talon from her right flank, he tries hard to grab hold of the left.

With a surge of fire and a double twist, Neria barely evades the second assault.

Pythius flips backward, escaping Neria's fire as he waits for another opportunity to maim. "Well, well, well." He continues to berate Neria. "Seems to me after all these years that you still haven't learned how to protect your blind side.

"Tsk, tsk. Whatever will I tell the horde?" he continues. "Neria, my cousin, who used to lead the strongest of us into battle with unrelenting strength and stealth, has become a mere servant to a weak, old king, who doesn't know the meaning of power or how to harness it for His glory."

Neria responds, "You speak of power, Pythius, but the only power or authority you have is what's been granted to you for a time. Your strength will evaporate like putrid water slipping out between the fingers of the righteous as they battle in prayer and in the field. It is vile and revolting, and one day Elyon will crush it at its source."

The reality of war fills the landscape. Lost lives, dismantled hope and agonizing cries. The atrocities committed in Elyon's name weigh heavily on the hearts of His warriors. Insurrection, mayhem and desecration play out as if on a stage within an invisible realm.

A fallen and impaled warrior cries out to Elyon to end his life. Elyon's mighty warriors push hard against the never-relenting horde of darkness.

"They just keep coming," one warrior shouts in horrific astonishment.

"Out of nowhere, it seems," says another.

"We fight until we fall, brother," answers another. "The victory is in Elyon's hands."

With the clash of metal and the twist of a knife, a warrior stumbles. His fighting comrade to the right screams as he trips over a decapitated body.

While he is on his knees, an arrow pierces his neck. His palor wanes as life flows out from his once vibrant body, soaking his garment in crimson red as he falls face down, whispering the only name that can save.

"Elyon!"

Looking out at the battle before him, Prince Amoz wills his warriors to fight without mercy, to kill and disfigure anyone draped in scarlet, for in this, Prince Amoz knows, lies their power.

Appealing to her Creator for words, Grace approaches the prince. "Your father says this battle is larger than what can be seen with the eye. There are forces at work not only on the battlefield but in your own mind, deceiving your will and emotions, twisting truth to lies. You see only what the darkness allows you to see, and you hear only what it wants you to.

"You call yourself a king," Grace continues cautiously, "but in reality you're like a marionette, doing the will of its maker without conscience thought or purpose. If you would only call on—"

Prince Amoz interrupts, scornfully staring into Grace's eyes. "Elyon? Is that what you were going to say? Call on the name of Elyon, and all your problems will fade away? Joy will replace depression, fullness will replace hunger, and love—that idealistic, overused word—is supposed to melt away judgmental hearts, full of gossip and slander."

Fuming with anger, the prince spits out the word. "Hypocrisy. I'm surrounded by it. I grew up surrounded by the righteous and so-called chosen of Elyon right here," he says as he motions around him, "inside these very walls, where love was supposed to reign. I listened as the court spread lies about my father, the one whom they had professed their loyalty to. I was there night after night, trying to soothe my mother from the hurt of judgment and scorn, Elyon's own children poured out under the guise of love.

"I watched her life slip away with every tear that fell. Sorrow and heartache were her only companions. It was hard for her to let go of the things that ultimately destroyed her, like depression, intimidation, and fear, because they were there when no one else was."

Prince Amoz looks into the expanse with fire and scorn in his eyes, as if searching for some tangible entity to draw strength to continue. "As much as my father and I petitioned and expected Elyon to heal her, He turned a deaf ear and let her die. My father, the king," he scoffs, turning once again to the screams and cries from the battlefield.

"Instead of anger toward Elyon, my father was at peace. In place of retaliation for these sanctimonious children, who drove her to take her life, he chose forgiveness. If that wasn't hard enough," the prince continues, "years later, after my father remarried, I witnessed my very religious stepmother discard her only child, my sibling. She threw her off a menacing crag due to imperfection and because she was born a daughter of Elyon. In that moment my heart became like a stone.

"You talk to me about Elyon's love and forgiveness. Where was His love when my mother called upon Him for deliverance from the pain these long-winded charlatans inflicted? I will never forgive a Creator who seemingly takes pleasure in the pain of one so innocent and gentle. Furthermore, I've vowed to destroy as many souls as I can by turning their hearts away from Elyon."

Smiling a sinister smile, the prince looks long into Grace's face. "I just never realized how easy the job would be."

Looking at Prince Amoz through tear-filled eyes, Grace sees not an evil prince bent on destroying all that is good. She sees a man-child, broken to the core. Grace reaches out to touch him ever so gently, hoping Prince Amoz will feel the Creator's love flowing through her.

Prince Amoz reacts violently as if burning coals have touched his skin. With his face flushed, sweat beads profusely on his forehead. His face contorts once again into something hideous and appalling. Without another word but a surreal growl, Prince Amoz picks Grace up and hurls her over the balcony.

With what feels like minutes of falling into the carnage below, hands trying to grasp something tangible, only seconds pass until she lands on the scaly and bleeding backside of Neria.

Drawing her sword from its sheath with unbridled determination and grit, Grace tries to direct Neria into the massacre unfolding below them. “I’m ready, Neria,” she shouts. “Take me into the rebellion, I’ll slice through this darkness with the strength of my sword sending the hored to hades gate. That will surely please Elyon.”

"Grace!" Neria pulls up, sharp with concern, landing on an overlook. "Our Creator does not delight in the death of anything He has created. Mercy and love always prevail. It grieves the heart of Elyon, as it should also grieve ours, that many are those whose choices will lead them to everlasting separation—far away from their Creator, who intended nothing but goodness."

Trying to understand the mystery of mercy and judgment from the same Creator who proclaims love is all is quite the paradox in Grace's thoughts. "There are so many, Neria," she says as she tearfully observes the innocents laying down their lives. "They appear to be so common in size and strength, not at all what I had imagined Elyon's warriors to be.

"In fact," Grace acknowledges, "they're not much different from me at all."

Neria smiles at Grace, knowing a seed of truth has taken root.

"It's so heartbreaking, Neria, to know the fallen will never experience victory, freedom from oppression. They will never receive recognition or win any kind of favor. It appears so meaningless."

"Meaningless? No, in this world, nothing is without meaning or purpose Grace, not even war." looking out into the hostility with sadness. "Their sacrifice, though great, will likely go unnoticed. They are among the forgotten, the misunderstood, the broken dregs of this world. They are the ones religious people look away from, lest a measure of empathy pricks their hearts.

"They have given their allegiance to one who is not only familiar with their suffering but who also walks beside them through the greatest of storms. This is one who gives them purpose for living, joy in the midst of pain, and a belief that they can be more than what they've become.

They will continue to fight against hypocrisy, abuse, and false truths without any praise, accolades, or medals until time bids them to lay down their swords and listen."

Perplexed, Grace asks, "Listen? Listen for what Neria?"

"A voice, wafting like a gentle breeze, immersing our soul in pure light. Calling us to a land that exist beyond the shadowy veil of this life."

Grace's inward thoughts are broken as her attention is drawn back to the fray. "There are so many dark lords. Do they never show mercy?"

Grace cringes as another warrior's life is sliced in two. With tears flowing, she begins to question why Elyon would allow such pain. "It looks hopeless, Neria. Just hopeless."

"Hopeless?" Neria asks. "For you or for Elyon?"

Feeling ashamed by Neria's quick rebuke, Grace lowers her head. "I'm sorry, Neria. We're losing. I just don't see a way out."

Goose bumps appear on Grace's arm. Moisture settles, causing the rocks she's holding onto to become cold and slippery. She positions herself so as not to fall. Placing one foot in front of a jagged rock protruding out of the hardened soil, she secures her position.

"Lift your eyes, Grace," Neria says with conviction. "See the faithfulness of our great King."

A softly falling mist, pure and transparent, is led by an unseen force through the battlefield and encircles the sons and daugthers of Elyon. New strength and boldness regenerate the weak and fallen.

Grace shouts with excitement as she pushes off from her unrelenting foothold, jumping up and down on her only leg, arms held high.

"Look, Neria," she says, pointing at the scene. "Do you see it? The battle's turning, but what is it that moves so softly and without resistance?"

Neria answers with reverence, "The breath of the Almighty, the one true God. The Lion of the tribe of Judah is here!"

With panic and confusion, the dark lords begin turning on one another, slicing and stabbing with fresh vengeance. Falling to their knees, they cry out for their god to save them. But all is quiet, for their gods cannot hear, see, or speak.

With a valiant shout of praise, Elyon's mighty warriors charge into battle with fresh tenacity and strength, claiming victory for their King.

Quickened footsteps echo in the silent corridor as they take King Tobiah through two iron doors leading onto the west balcony. Seeing his son, the king is filled with mercy and love. "Amoz," he calls out, trying to reconcile.

The prince turns to face the familiar voice and shouts, "You were placed in that tower, and there you were to remain by my orders."

The prince enraged with resentment and animosity. "Imbeciles, my soldiers, who can't even keep one insignificant king locked up."

"Not even you, Amoz, can lock up a person's spirit, and it's with this that I do my battle," King Tobiah replies. "It's never too late for redemption. Lay your anger aside, Amoz.

With mercy and truth we can lead Elyon's children in peace against the darkness."

Stepping up to his father, the prince trembles with deep-seated bitterness as he pushes his finger into his father's chest. "I despise everything about you. You're not a king but some passive, indifferent, little worm that succumbs to pressure around him with sympathy and prayers. You're a weak creature, who could have had it all—adoration, treasure, the power to give life or take it.

"It's too late for you but not for me. I've discovered the hidden scrolls, Father, which will lead me to the forbidden realm. It's been granted to me that I shall rule supremely—if not now, then soon. Everyone will bow before me, even you, Father, and your precious Elyon."

"At what cost, Amoz? At what cost to you?" The king's voice shakes with emotion. "If you build your kingdom on nothing but pride, it will surely crumble. Then you will be left with nothing, not even your soul."

Smiling his sinister smile, Prince Amoz turns, making his way to Pythius and leaving the king with parting words. "l will crush your kingdom one day, Father. I will be most powerful."

Saddened and grieved in heart, the king watches as his son disappears into the blackness of his own soul.

King Tobiah, seated securely on his throne, addresses his court and admonishes humbled hearts to break up their fallow ground and build a new foundation where love is the cornerstone.

“As for you, Grace,” the king says smiling, “I look upon a mighty warrior, faithful and dedicated to the service of Elyon, who has hopefully learned that being a warrior is not dependent on physical strength or form. Nor does it depend on perfect speech or a great mind, but it requires only a heart submitted to the one true King, who calls all of us to become more than we could ever imagine in ourselves. On behalf of the kingdom and myself, accept this gift of mobility. Then perhaps you won’t be falling through any more castle windows.”

The beauty beckons Grace from the valley below and the snow-capped peaks of the mountain range. A herd of docile sheep graze on the highlands, ever secure, while knowing the eye of their shepherd is keeping watch.

"There is something beautiful and tranquil about a land submitted to goodness and peace; if only it could remain like this forever," Grace whispers in quiet and reverent tones.

"Someday," Neria responds, "all will be as it should be. But for now, we are called to war against an invisible force and not to lose heart."

"I fear we haven't seen the last of Prince Amoz," Grace confides to Neria. "The evil that surrounds him seems greater than we can even fathom. How do we fight against something we can't even touch or see with our eyes?"

Neria responds. "Every moment of every day, we renew our minds.

Getting to know the heart of the Creator will make it easier to identify the counterfeit, even if it comes dressed as a prince. We must press on, for, in the heat of the battle, it's too late to prepare."

Looking out from a darkened and undisclosed cavern within the mountainside, Prince Amoz conspires within the shadows of his own mind, devising plans of treachery and deception to bring down his clever and savvy new foe. He begins to calculate how to render her unsuitable for any calling other than his own.

"Rest and renew your strength, my friend," Prince Amos says, addressing Pythius.

"We have plans to make and battles to win. I will be as He," he says, speaking of Elyon, "in brilliance and opulence." "I will conquer one soul at a time, beginning with Grace."

After quiet reflection, familiar surroundings bring Grace back to the reality of lessons yet to be learned. "Aw, Neria," Grace complains, "must we go back to Aloysius? He tires me out until I have nothing left to give."

"Which is why you must continue with your training. There is no one better suited to teach you how to stand firm against the enemy," Neria responds.

Grace appeals to Neria. "I just thought after Elyon's victory, we might take a rest—you know, like a holiday."

"A holiday!" shouts an imposing Aloysius, who emerges from his cave. "You have been a witness to one small victory against the horde of darkness, and already you wish to take a holiday? You have much to learn, little warrior, and what better place than in the dust, where we began? Now, suppose we start where we left off."

Challenging Grace, Aloysius readies his stance.

Up above, unbeknownst to the three warriors, in the overgrown foliage of a mountain precipice, Elyon is watching. Filled with a love that is immeasurable, patient, and forgiving His spirit gently calls back to Himself those who have long forgotten Him.

Mercy and grace flood the valley, where hate and bitterness once prevailed. Longing to walk beside us, calling us His own and molding us into something greater than we can see in ourselves…a great and mighty warrior.

The Battle Continues...

Origins of Names

Aloysius	–	Famous Warrior
Gender	–	Masculine
Usage	–	English
Pron.	–	al-o-iSH-es
Origin	–	Ancient Germanic, French, Medieval

Amoz	–	Strong, to carry, burden
Gender	–	Masculine
Usage	–	Biblical
Origin	–	Hebrew, Latin, Greek, English

Grace	–	Unmerited favor of God towards man
Gender	–	Feminine
Usage	–	Biblical, English, Middle Ages, Latin
Origin	–	Latin, Old French, Biblical

Neria	–	Burning light of God
Gender	–	Feminine
Usage	–	Hebrew (Modern)
Pron.	–	NER-yah
Origin	–	Hebrew

Pythius – Medieval-style dragon means "to rot"
Gender – Masculine/Feminine
Usage – Ancient Greek Mythology
Pron. – Phyth-i-us
Origin - Greek

Tobiah – YAHWEH is Good
Gender – Masculine
Usage – Biblical
Pron. – to-BIE-a
Origin – Ancient Hebrew

God Most High

Gender Masculine
Usage Biblical
Pron. El-yon
Origin Hebrew

Printed in the United States
By Bookmasters